WHY DOESN'T THE SUN BURN OUT?

By VICKI COBB, WITH ILLUSTRATIONS BY TED ENIK

Why Doesn't the Earth Fall Up?
  and other not such dumb questions about motion

Why Can't You Unscramble an Egg?
  and other not such dumb questions about matter

ALSO BY VICKI COBB

Gobs of Goo
Lots of Rot
The Monsters Who Died
More Power to You!
Skyscraper Going Up!
The Trip of a Drip
This Place is COLD
This Place is DRY

WHY DOESN'T THE SUN BURN OUT?

and other not such dumb questions about energy

BY VICKI COBB

illustrated by Ted Enik

LODESTAR BOOKS   DUTTON   NEW YORK

Library of Congress Cataloging-in-Publication Data

Cobb, Vicki.
  Why doesn't the sun burn out?: and other not such dumb
questions about energy / by Vicki Cobb; illustrated by Ted
Enik.—1st ed.
      p.   cm.
  "Lodestar books."
  Summary: Presents nine questions on different kinds of
energy, such as heat, kinetic, and chemical energy, and
their relation to matter.
  ISBN 0-525-67301-6
  1. Force and energy—Juvenile literature. [1. Force
and energy. 2. Questions and answers.] I. Enik, Ted,
ill. II. Title
QC73.4.C63 1990   89-37467
531'.6—dc20   CIP
                                                 AC

Published in the United States by Lodestar Books,
an affiliate of Dutton Children's Books,
a division of Penguin Books USA Inc.

Published simultaneously in Canada by
McClelland & Stewart, Toronto

Editor: Virginia Buckley
Printed in the U.S.A.   First Edition
10 9 8 7 6 5 4 3 2 1

Contents

What Does It Take To Move a Piano?

A piano is a heavy object that resists being moved. The resistance of an object to being moved is called *inertia*. A piano won't move unless it is pushed hard enough to overcome its inertia. The push also has to be strong enough to overcome the friction between the piano and the floor. If you want to lift the piano, then the force you use has to overcome its weight. Weight is the force of gravity on an object.

Whenever a force moves something like a piano, scientists say that *work* has been done. If you try to move a piano, no matter how much you huff and puff, you haven't done any work if it doesn't move. Scientists are very particular about the idea of work. Work is accomplished only when matter is moved.

Now the question is, What does it take to do work? The answer sounds simple, but there are many ways of thinking about this. It takes *energy* to do work. Energy can come from many sources. It can come from muscles, or an engine, or a wall socket. Whenever you see an object changing its speed or moving against a force, it's because of energy. The energy of motion is called *kinetic energy,* and all moving objects have it.

9

How Is a Wound-Up Spring Like the Top of a Waterfall?

Both a wound-up spring in a watch or a toy and the water at the top of a waterfall have stored energy. Stored energy isn't doing any work. When the water falls, the energy is released as kinetic energy. If the water falls on a water wheel, it makes the wheel turn. The kinetic energy of a turning water wheel can then move a millstone to grind flour or turn a turbine to generate electricity. The kinetic energy is now doing useful work. When a spring unwinds, it also can do useful work. It can move the hands of a watch or make a toy car run. Machines are inventions that use energy for useful work.

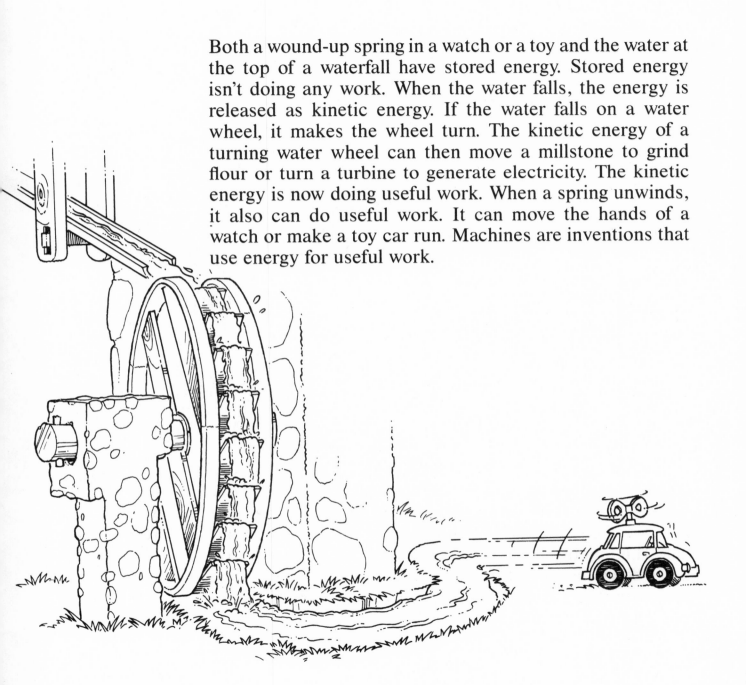

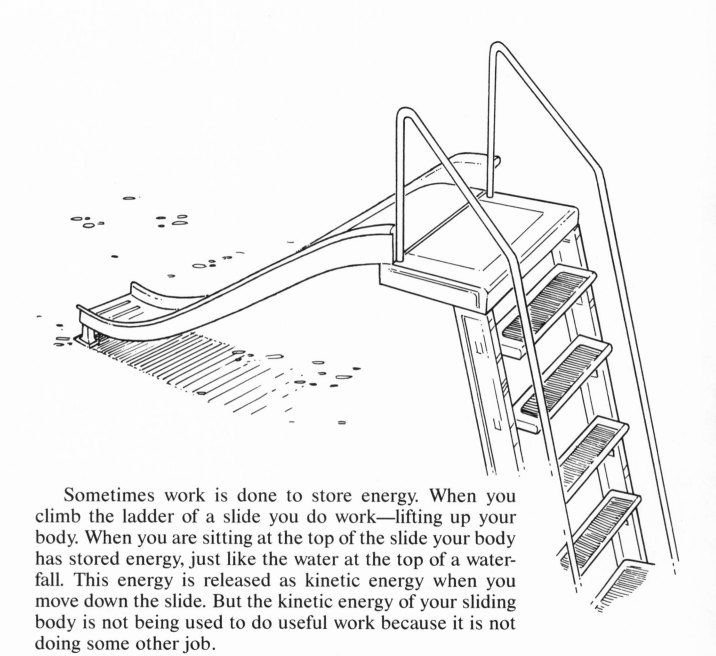

Sometimes work is done to store energy. When you climb the ladder of a slide you do work—lifting up your body. When you are sitting at the top of the slide your body has stored energy, just like the water at the top of a waterfall. This energy is released as kinetic energy when you move down the slide. But the kinetic energy of your sliding body is not being used to do useful work because it is not doing some other job.

Do Hot Things Weigh More Than Cold Things?

14

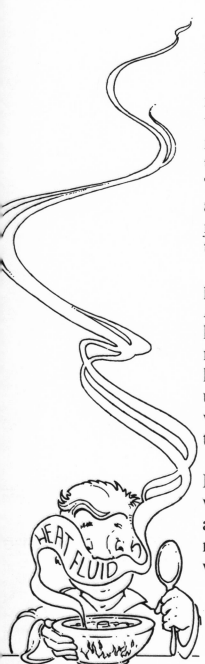

People used to think that heat was a kind of fluid. They believed that when things cooled off the heat fluid escaped into the air. As a result, they believed that hot things should weigh more than cold things. But when they did experiments weighing hot things and cold things to see if hot things weighed more, the scales didn't show any difference. They made better and better scales, but they still didn't see any difference. An object weighed exactly the same no matter how hot or cold it was. People needed a new way to think about heat.

Count Benjamin Thompson Rumford was one of the people who tried to measure the weight of heat. He was an American who moved to England after the American Revolution. He had the job of supervising the making of cannons. He noticed that the metal of a brass cannon got very hot when it was being hollowed out. The motion of the tool used to hollow out the cannon caused the heat. Rumford was the first person to think that motion and heat might be the same thing.

Are motion and heat the same thing? See for yourself. Rub your hands together quickly and see how they get warmer. Is the opposite true? Can heat produce motion and do work? You bet! The steam engine is one kind of machine that changes the heat energy released by burning wood into the steam that runs a locomotive.

Fuels also have stored energy, which is sometimes called *chemical energy*. Chemical energy is released as heat and light when the fuel burns during a chemical reaction.

So the question of whether hot things weigh more than cold things was not so dumb, after all. It led to the important idea that one kind of energy can change into another kind. Energy can take many forms. In addition to heat, kinetic, and chemical energy, other kinds of energy are sound, light, and electricity.

Some of the devices that change one kind of energy into another are a toaster, which changes electricity into heat; TV, which turns electricity into light and sound; an alarm clock, which transforms kinetic energy into sound; and a car, which turns chemical energy (burning fuel) into heat and, in turn, into kinetic energy.

Electricity is one of the easiest kinds of energy for us to use. But usable electricity doesn't exist in nature. It has to be made from other kinds of energy. Falling water or burning coal or oil is used to make electricity at power plants.

Does Water That Boils Faster Cook Faster?

If you have a cooking thermometer, you can watch what happens when you heat water in a pot. (Don't try to boil water without having an adult present.) As the pot sits over the flame on the burner, the water begins moving. The temperature goes up, and the water moves faster and faster. Tiny bubbles start forming on the bottom of the pot. These are not air bubbles but water that has changed into a gas called *steam*.

The tiny steam bubbles rise to the surface as the water starts to boil. The thermometer reads 212 degrees on the Fahrenheit scale and 100 degrees on the Celsius scale. The bubbles get larger and the water moves more and more rapidly. Finally it reaches a rolling boil. The temperature stays at exactly 212 degrees Fahrenheit, or 100 degrees Celsius, and never changes!

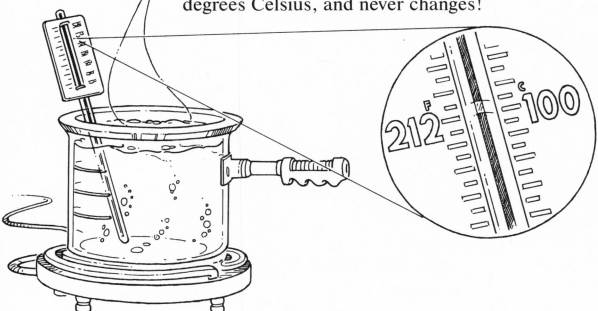

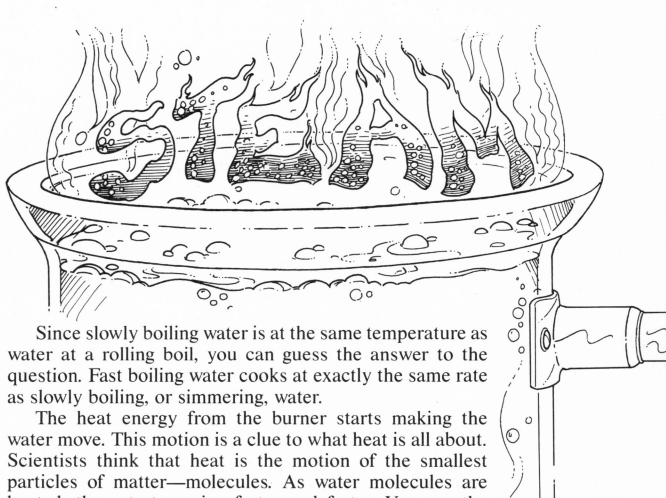

Since slowly boiling water is at the same temperature as water at a rolling boil, you can guess the answer to the question. Fast boiling water cooks at exactly the same rate as slowly boiling, or simmering, water.

The heat energy from the burner starts making the water move. This motion is a clue to what heat is all about. Scientists think that heat is the motion of the smallest particles of matter—molecules. As water molecules are heated, they start moving faster and faster. You see the temperature rise. When the temperature reaches 212 degrees F, or 100 degrees C, the water molecules are moving fast enough to escape from the water's surface as steam. Now the heat energy changes water into steam. But the temperature of the water won't change until it has all been changed to steam.

How Does a Pot Holder Work?

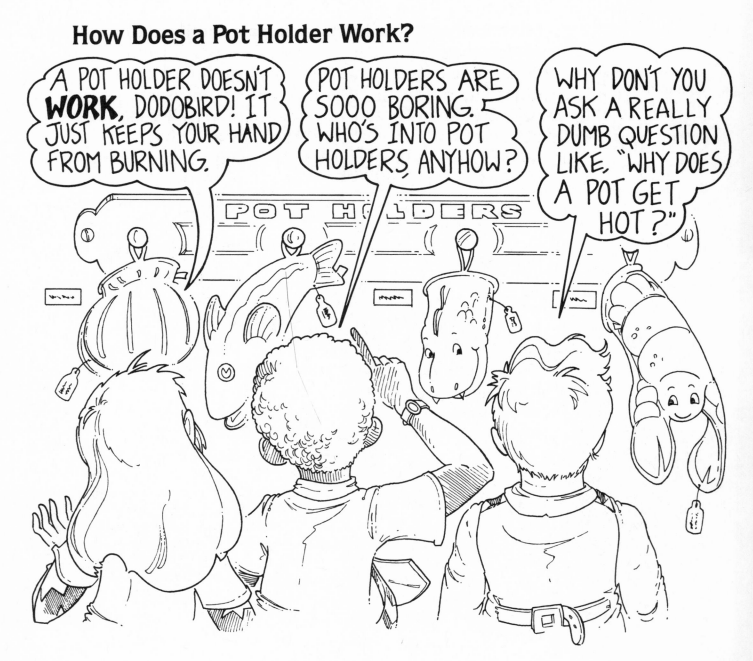

More energy is needed to overcome the inertia of some objects than others. The same thing is true of molecules. It takes more energy to move certain kinds of molecules than other kinds. The speed of molecules is measured as temperature. Some materials get hot more easily than others because their molecules are moved more easily. Metals get hot very easily. For this reason they are called *heat conductors.* A metal pot handle can get too hot to touch. If you put a metal spoon in a cup of hot coffee, it will soon begin to feel warm. Try this and see.

Other materials absorb heat without getting hot. These materials are called *insulators.* Most nonmetals and air are good insulators. Fabric is a good insulator. When you wrap a hot pot handle in a pot holder, the pot holder acts as an insulator. Your hand is protected.

Styrofoam is another good heat insulator. Experiment and see for yourself. Get a paper cup, a Styrofoam cup, and a foil baking cup. Put an ice cube in each. See which ice cube melts fastest. The best insulator protects the cube from heat in the air.

IF THERE'S NO HEAT CONDUCTOR AROUND A HOT DRINK THE DRINK STAYS HOT.

A THERMOS BOTTLE KEEPS THINGS WARM OR COLD BY INSULATING WITH A VACUUM.

Why Isn't the Sky Green or Yellow?
Why Blue?

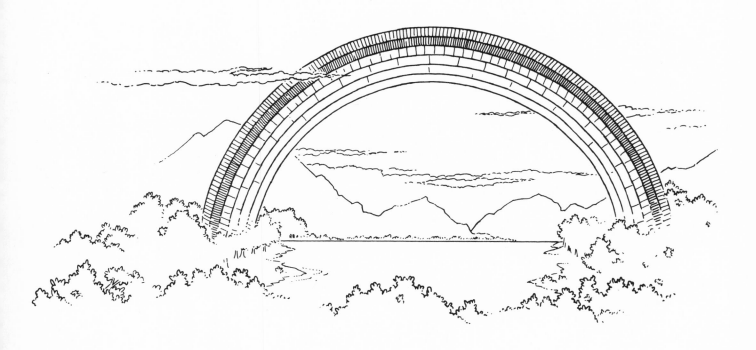

First of all, the sky is black at night, when there is no sunlight. So the color of the sky depends on light, which is a kind of energy. Light from the sun appears to be white. But you can see a clue to its real nature when a rainbow forms. A rainbow is sunlight broken up into many different colors: violet, blue, green, yellow, orange, and red. All these different colors make up the *spectrum*. When we see the whole spectrum combined, we are seeing white light.

Try this out for yourself. All you need is a cereal dish filled with water about two inches deep, a small hand mirror, a sheet of white paper, and a sunny day.

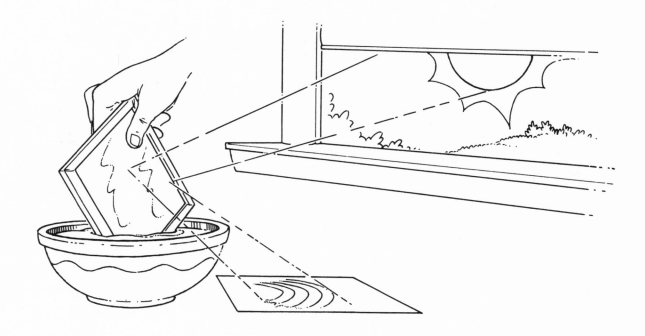

Put the dish of water in the sunlight. Put one end of the mirror in the water. You can easily make a bright spot of light reflect off the mirror onto the piece of paper. Then change the tilt of the mirror until you capture a spectrum on your piece of paper. The red and yellow will be at the top edge and the green, blue, and violet at the bottom.

Matter reflects light. A mirror reflects almost all the light that strikes it, while a red object reflects only red light. Air particles reflect light in all directions, because air scatters light. The colors that are scattered the most are violet and blue. Our eyes are not as sensitive to violet as to blue, so we see the sky as blue.

Who Ever Heard of Light You Can't See?

The only way we can know about energy is by what it does to matter. For example, energy moves matter, raises its temperature, changes it from a solid to a liquid or from a liquid to a gas, and changes its color. We see light because we have nerves in our eyes that react to it. But our eyes are not able to detect the entire spectrum. The light our eyes cannot see must be detected in some other way. The trick is to find a substance on which light can be recorded, like film in a camera.

Film in a camera is coated with a substance that turns dark when light strikes it. Patterns of light and shadow from the real world show up as pictures on film. Can film detect light that our eyes are not able to see? Absolutely! One person who detected invisible light rays was a French scientist named Antoine-Henri Becquerel. In 1896, Becquerel wrapped photographic film in black paper. He put a mineral containing uranium on top of the wrapped film. When he developed the film, he found a cloudy area under the mineral. The mineral was giving off invisible rays that could pass through paper. These invisible rays are called *radioactivity*. Photographic film shows that there is light we cannot see at both the red and the violet ends of the spectrum.

The invisible light next to the violet end is called *ultraviolet*. Ultraviolet light from the sun will cause your skin to become sunburned. Next to the red end of the spectrum is the invisible *infrared* light. Infrared light makes objects warm. Black objects absorb more infrared light than do white objects. See for yourself. Put a sheet of black paper and a sheet of white paper in bright sunlight. After five minutes, feel both pieces of paper. Which one feels warmer?

X rays are invisible rays next to ultraviolet in the spectrum. They can pass through the soft parts of your body and take pictures of your bones.

Microwaves are next to infrared rays. In a microwave oven, energy from the microwave makes water molecules move faster, so food gets hot and quickly cooks.

What Does Energy Weigh?

For many years scientists believed that only matter had weight. They thought that energy was completely different from matter and weighed nothing. Then, at the beginning of the twentieth century, Albert Einstein came along and changed the way everyone thought about matter and energy.

Einstein said that matter and energy were the same thing. Energy equals matter that has been multiplied by a huge number, bigger than you can imagine. Enormous amounts of energy can be released from a tiny bit of matter. So, according to Einstein, energy weighs so little that it can't be measured, only calculated. The important thought is that energy, which equals matter, weighs something. Only certain kinds of matter change into energy in nature.

One type of matter that changes into energy is a radioactive material such as uranium. Little pieces of uranium atoms break off and release energy in the process. The invisible rays photographed by Antoine-Henri Becquerel are this type of energy. Some of the rays are like X rays and can pass through skin into the body where they can cause harm. Uranium atoms fall apart all by themselves. But to make an atom bomb, scientists deliberately split atoms. Uranium atoms are split into bigger pieces than what would chip off naturally, so even more matter changes into huge amounts of energy.

Nuclear energy, the energy that comes from splitting uranium atoms, is both heat energy and invisible light in the form of dangerous radiation. Nuclear power plants use the heat to make steam that generates electricity. Radioactivity from uranium, the fuel for nuclear power plants, is dangerous. Extra care must be taken so that deadly radiation doesn't escape into the air.

Some people are against nuclear energy because of its dangers. Everyone wants electricity, but almost every kind of energy used to make electricity has problems.

Where dams are built to make waterfalls, the falling water generates electricity at hydroelectric plants. But the lakes formed by the dams cover over valuable land. So some people are against these dams. Other power plants burn oil and gas. There is a limited amount of these clean-burning fuels. Some plants burn coal. The smoke from these plants can cause acid rain that pollutes the land. People protest about fuel-burning plants. What happens when oil and gas are used up? Scientists are thinking about ways to use the wind, the tides, the sun, or the heat in the ocean to make electricity. But they haven't found practical answers yet.

Why Doesn't the Sun Burn Out?

The secret of the sun's constant energy is that it is not fire. A fire is a chemical reaction that lasts until all the fuel is used up. The sun's energy is a kind of nuclear energy. Atoms of hydrogen, the lightest gas in the universe, fuse together on the sun to make atoms of helium, the second lightest gas in the universe. A helium atom weighs slightly less than the two atoms of hydrogen that made it. This difference in mass is lost, and is released as energy— tremendous amounts of energy.

The hydrogen bomb, which is far more powerful than the atom bomb, depends on *nuclear fusion*. Nuclear fusion takes place at extremely hot temperatures, such as those created by an atom bomb. In fact, the trigger for the hydrogen bomb is an atom bomb. The amount of heat energy released by fusion is so great that all matter that comes near it is vaporized. Scientists have not yet found a way to use fusion for peaceful purposes.

Our sun is about four and a half billion years old. Scientists figure that it will continue to give off energy steadily for another five billion years or so, before it goes into its old age.

Index